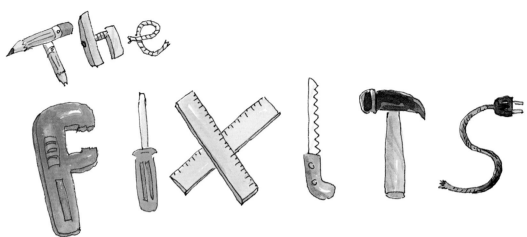

# The Fixits

Anne Mazer

Illustrated by Paul Meisel

HYPERION BOOKS FOR CHILDREN · NEW YORK

One day, the Fixits arrived.

"888 Teapot Drive? What can we fix for you today, kids?"

Augusta held out a cracked plate. "It was an accident." She shrugged.

"It's our mother's favorite," I added.

"We're the Fixits. We fix anything. Accidents happen. We take care of them."

"Uh-oh," said Ed. "You never could throw straight, Tom."

"Easy does it. Accidents happen. We can fix it. Just give me a broom and some glue."

Ed spread glue over the floor in a big circle, then Tom swept the broken pieces onto it.

"The broom is stuck," I said. Augusta grabbed a ball and some string. "Let's tie a ball on it," she yelled, "and play punchball!"

"It's ruined!" I cried.

"Easy does it. Accidents happen. We can fix it. We just need a saw."

Whoosh! The floor fell in.

"Maybe we can hang a rope ladder," my little sister said, "and swing like Tarzan."

I frowned. "What if someone falls down?"

"Easy does it. Accidents happen. We can fix it. Tom, bring over the wood and nails."

"Tom, hand me that hammer."
"*Uh-oh,*" said Tom.
"Easy does it. Accidents happen.
We can fix it. Give me that wrench."

"*Oops,*" said Ed, as the wall crumbled. Augusta's eyes lit up. "Let's build a tunnel."

"Mom won't like it!" I said.

"Easy does it. Accidents happen," said Ed. "We can fix it. Just hand me a couple of those two-by-fours."

"Whoops," said Tom, as the wall collapsed and the roof fell in.

"I can fly my kite in the living room!" Augusta cried.

I held up my hand. "I feel a raindrop," I said.

"Easy does it. Accidents happen. We can fix it. All we need are a ladder and a patch."

"King of the mountain!"
my little sister yelled. *"Wheeee!"*

"Our mother is *not* going to
like this," I said.

"Easy does it," said the Fixits.

"Accidents happen. We can fix it.
We just need a couple of crowbars."

Tom and Ed pried up the floor, and the rubble spilled into the basement.

"Hooray! Let's dig caves!" Augusta cried.

I sifted through the dust. "Maybe we can vacuum it up?"

"Easy does it, kids. Accidents happen. We can fix it. Just give me a jackhammer."

"*Uh-oh,*" said the Fixits.
"Landslide!" yelled Augusta.
"Accidents happen," said
the Fixits. "We can fix your
house. Easy does it."

The Fixits ran to their
truck. They pulled out an
eggbeater, a lawn mower,
a knife, a fork, a typewriter,
a clock, a pail, a pair of
scissors, and a camera.

Our mother drove up.

"Mom!" Augusta called. "We cracked a plate!"

"Oh, accidents happen," Mom said.

"We can fix anything," said the Fixits.

To our friends on the block:
Madeline, Calvin, Lisle, and Carter.
— A. M.

Text © 1999 by Anne Mazer.
Illustrations © 1999 by Paul Meisel.

First Edition
3 5 7 9 10 8 6 4 2

The artwork for each picture is prepared using watercolors.
This book is set in 16-point Tiepolo.

Library of Congress Cataloging-in-Publication Data
Mazer, Anne.
The Fixits / Anne Mazer; illustrated by Paul Meisel.-1st ed.
p. cm.
Summary: After Michael and Augusta break their mother's favorite plate, they call the Fixits, who shatter more than the china.
ISBN 0-7868-0213-8 (trade)- ISBN 0-7868-2202-3 (lib.)
[1. Repairing-Fiction. 2. Brothers and sisters-Fiction. 3. Humorous stories.] I. Meisel, Paul, ill. II. Title.
PZ7.M7396Fi 1998
[E]-dc20    98-13599